Charlie Blue Berry
Fipple Berry

DAVID FLEMING

iUniverse, Inc.
Bloomington

Charlie Blue Berry Fipple Berry

This is a work of fiction. All of the characters, names, incidents, organizations, and dialogue in this novel are either the products of the author's imagination or are used fictitiously.

iUniverse books may be ordered through booksellers or by contacting:

iUniverse
1663 Liberty Drive
Bloomington, IN 47403
www.iuniverse.com
1-800-Authors (1-800-288-4677)

ISBN: 978-1-4759-1944-8 (sc)
ISBN: 978-1-4759-1945-5 (hc)
ISBN: 978-1-4759-1946-2 (ebk)

Library of Congress Control Number: 2012907726

Printed in the United States of America

iUniverse rev. date: 05/10/2012

In the land of Sweet Smellums lives a little boy named Charlie Blue Berry Fipple Berry. He lives with his Mother Mrs. Candy Pie Fipple Berry, and his Father, Mr. Grape Berry Fipple Berry.

Charlie Blue Berry Fipple Berry is a quiet happy little boy, but today he is really happy, because today is the last day of school.

Charlie Blue Berry Fipple Berry jumped out of bed and shouted . . . . "yippie . . . . yippie it's the last day of school"

Charlie Blue Berry Fipple Berry is in the 6th grade at Lemon Berry Elementary School. No one could be happier than little Charlie Blue Berry Fipple Berry. Charlie Blue Berry Fipple Berry worked hard all year long to get good grades in school. Some days he did well, and other days not so well. No one is happier today like Charlie Blue Berry Fipple Berry because, his teacher told him his final grades were very good, and he would go to the 7th grade.

Today is the very last day of school, and for Charlie Blue Berry Fipple Berry that means, playing, having fun, swimming and doing all kind of fun things, with his best friend, Norry Norris Fruit Bean.

Charlie Blue Berry Fipple Berry was an average little Hedgehog. He was just like all the other little ones in Sweet Smellums. All year long Charlie Blue Berry Fipple Berry had to learn many lessons in being good and doing the right things, even if others around him were doing the wrong things.

Sometimes Charlie Blue Berry Fipple Berry made mistakes and got into trouble, and sometimes Charlie Blue Berry Fipple Berry did the right things and stayed out of trouble.

Charlie Blue Berry Fipple Berry had dreamed of this day for a long, long time and now that day was here. Every year when school lets out for the summer that means that Charlie Blue Berry Fipple Berry would be a year older, and his parents would allow him to do more things. Charlie Blue Berry Fipple Berry would feel sad when a lot of the little ones were allowed to go places and do things that he could not do.

There were three things Charlie Blue Berry Fipple Berry loved to do and that was Blueberry muffins, fishing and playing with his best friend Norry Norris Fruit Bean.

Norry Norris is a very big polar Bear, not as big as his Brothers and Sisters, and not as big as a tree, but Norry Norris is very big. Because Charlie Blue Berry Fipple Berry is little, a lot of the ones at school would pick on Charlie and call him names. That used to hurt Charlie Blue Berry Fipple Berry's feelings, until the day he met Norry Norris Fruit Bean and they became friends.

Charlie Blue Berry Fipple Berry sat on the edge of the bed thinking about what to wear on his last day of school. It had to be something very, special.

"I know what I'll wear . . . . Charlie Blue Berry Fipple Berry said to himself?"

He reached in his closet and brought out his new Blue shirt his Mother had given him, and his Blue suspenders his Father had given him. "These are going to be my very, very special clothes for the last day of school . . . Charlie Blue Berry Fipple Berry said smiling."

Charlie Blue Berry Fipple Berry loved the color Blue, it was his favorite color. Everything Charlie Blue Berry Fipple Berry had was Blue, all except a bright red scarf that Norry Norris gave him. Norry Norris told Charlie Blue Berry Fipple Berry when he gave him the red scarf that, "it's always good to try something new, try something new".

Charlie Blue Berry Fipple Berry washed his face, behind his ears, fluffed his hair, put on his favorite blue jacket and red scarf and ran downstairs.

Good morning Momma, Charlie Blue Berry Fipple Berry said. "Well good morning back to you" . . . Charlie's Mother said with a big smile.

Charlie's Mother picked him up and gave him a hug and a kiss.

Guess what Momma,
Charlie Blue Berry Fipple Berry said?

Charlie's Mother wondered . . . . uumm what could it be? Then she looked at him and said, "Could it be that today is the last day of school?"

Charlie Blue Berry Fipple Berry said "awww Momma, how did you guess?"

Charlie's Momma said, "Since you started school, I have counted the days and today is the last day of school for you Charlie.

Charlie's Mother made Charlie a very special treat to go along with his breakfast. Charlie Blue Berry Fipple Berry loved Fresh Blue Berry Muffins. He could eat Blue Berry muffins for breakfast and he could eat them for lunch; and he could eat them for dinner . . . .

Charlie Blue Berry Fipple Berry could eat them all day, and all night. This was his most favorite food to eat. Charlie's Mother was always reminding Charlie Blue Berry Fipple Berry, that a growing little boy or girl needs more to eat, than just the things they loved. Growing little boys and girls needed things that were good for them too.

Charlie's Mother made Oatmeal with fresh Blue Berries, Blue Berry Muffins and slice Apples with milk.

Charlie's Mother pulled a fresh, hot pan of Blue Berry muffins from the oven, and said to Charlie Blue Berry Fipple Berry . . . .

"here you are Charlie, oatmeal with Blue Berries, Blue Berry muffins, and a big glass of milk with Blue Berries".

Charlie, said "but Momma where are the apple slices?" Charlie's Mother said, Charlie, I have a very special apple just for you in the apple cupboard, while you were at school yesterday; I picked one special for you . . .

Charlie Blue Berry Fipple Berry sat in front of the fresh Blue Berry Muffins, oatmeal with Blue Berries and milk with Blue Berries and apple slices and ate, until his plate was clean.

Charlie Blue Berry Fipple Berry reached out his hand for a few more Blue Berry muffins, and his mother said . . . . "Charlie, I think you have had enough Blue Berry muffins." Charlie's Mother always baked extra food for Mrs. Fruit Jelly Goose who lived in the cherry house down the street. Mrs. Fruit Jelly Goose was very poor and had 3 new Gooslings to feed.

Charlie's Mother told Charlie Blue Berry Fipple Berry
how important it was to give whatever you can to
others who are in need.

The clock in the kitchen began to coo-coo-chee-coo. Charlie's Mother said as she was going upstairs . . ." you better get going or you will be late for your last day of school, and you do not want to keep Norry Norris Fruit Bean waiting.

Remember Charlie; don't eat your lunch before you get to school, and save your lunch for lunch time.

Charlie Blue Berry Fipple Berry loved Blueberry muffins so much, that he sneaked more Blue Berry muffins from the pan and stuffed them in his pockets!

Charlie Blue Berry Fipple Berry, grabbed his books, and ran out the door. Charlie Blue Berry Fipple Berry was in such a hurry to get out of the house before his Mother could find out what he had done, that he did not even say good bye.

Charlie Blue Berry Fipple Berry ran out the house, down the hill and over Mufffinville creek . . . . Untill he met his friend Norry Norris Fruit Bean.

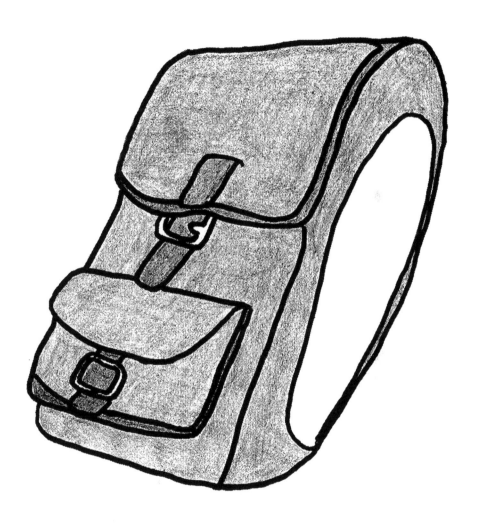

Norry Norris Fruit Bean and Charlie Blue Berry Fipple
Berry walked to school together since they were in
kindergarden. Sometimes, Norry Norris Fruit Bean
would throw Charlie Blue Berry Fipple Berry on his
back if it was raining, so that Charlie Blue Berry Fipple
Berry could stay dry.

"Hey Charlie Charlie, today is the last day of school, the last day of school"!

Hi ya . . . . Norry Norriy, Charlie Blue Berry Fipple Berry said laughing at Norry Norris Fruit Bean".

"Charlie, Charlie why are you always laugh at me when I talk, when I talk?

I'm sorry Norry Norriy I don't mean to, I't just sounds so funny when you say things twice.

Oh that's okay Charlie Blue Berry Fipple Berry, Fipple Berry, grunted Norry Norris.

Charlie Blue Berry Fipple Berry said, I had a special breakfast this morning of oatmeal with Blue Berries and Blueberry muffins and sliced apples, what did you have Norry Norry?

Norry Norris Fruit Bean said, I had ten waffles with cherry syrup, five bowls of choclate covered cherry ceral, and two big mugs of cherry orange juice.

"Wow Norry Norry, you sure can eat, Charlie Blue Berry Fipple Berry said holding his stomach"! Aww sucks Charlie that was just a snack, just a snack. I tried to sneak two more stacks of waffles when my Mother's back was turned but she saw me and said it was not nice to take things without asking, without asking.

Charlie Blue Berry Fipple Berry started thinking about what he had done by sneaking the Blue Berry Muffins. Charlie Blue Berry Fipple Berry was thinking about how his Mother told him not to take anymore because they were for Mrs. Fruit Jelly Goose, and began to feel sad.

"We have waited all year for this day Charlie Blue Berry Fipple Berry, all year for this day, said Norry Norris Fruit Bean as he smelled the Blue Berry Muffins in Charlie Blue Berry Fipple Berry's back pack and jacket pockets.

Umm What's to eat, what's to eat Charlie?

Just a few Blueberry muffins I took . . . I mean Momma gave me before I left, but I ate so many at breakfast I can't eat another one.

Over the hill towards the edge of Muffinville to Ousey Bousey Mousey's barn the two walked . . . .

Every morning on their way to school, Charlie Blue Berry Fipple Berry and Norry Norris Fruit Bean stopped at Ousey Bousey Mousey's barn and ate whatever snacks they had in their back packs. Norry Norris Fruit Bean could not wait because he was so hungry and the smell of those Blueberry muffins coming from Charlie Blue Berry Fipple Berry's back pack and jacket pockets were smelling so good that Norry Norris grabbed Charlie Blue Berry Fipple Berry, flipped Charlie Blue Berry Fipple Berry on his back and ran really fast.

When they reached the barn door, they opened it, and saw Ousey Bousey Mousey sitting on a bale of hay and eating a slice of Lemon cheese pie . . . .

Ousey Bousey Mousey looked up at them said
g-g-g-good m-m-morning.

"Hi back, hi back", said Norry Norris Fruit Bean, pulling
out the Strawberry and pancakes, and tuna salad from
his bag.

Charlie Blue Berry Fipple Berry came in and sat down and pulled his pack off his shoulders. Charlie Blue Berry Fipple Berry gave Norry Norris Fruit Bean all of the Blue Berry muffins he took from home, he even gave Norry Norris the ones that his Mother gave to him for a snack.

Well, what's b-b-bothering you C-C-Charlie B-B-B-Blue B-B-Berry F-F-Fipple B-B-Berry, said Ousey Bousey Mousey?

Aww Charlie is not bothered, not bothered Ousey, said Norry Norris Fruit Bean, (stuffing his mouth with strawberries and pancakes and tuna salad)

Charlie ate too much at breakfast this morning, at breakfast this morning.

Ousey Bousey Mousey looked over at Charlie Blue Berry Fipple Berry, and told him to come on over and have a seat, besides him, that he had the cure for a stomach that had too much food in it.

Ousey Bousey Mousey gave Charlie Blue Berry Fipple Berry a big chunk of Limburger Cheese. Charlie Blue Berry Fipple Berry took one smell of the cheese that Ousey Bousey Mousey was trying to give him and said . . . .

Ousey Bousey Mousey, this cheese does not smell so good!

Don't knock it until you t-t-tried it, T-T-T-This is the g-g-good s-s-stuff . . . . said Ousey Bousey Mousey . . . (Picking his teeth with a straw)

Norry Norris Fruit Bean looked over at Charlie Blue Berry Fipple Berry, and said . . . ." are there any more snacks in the back pack, in the back pack?

Charlie Blue Berry Fipple Berry reached into his left pocket, then into his right pocket and said . . . no more Norry Norry.

Yum, yum said Norry, with syrup dripping from his chin and Blueberries all around his mouth.

Even when Charlie Blue Berry Fipple Berry gave the muffins away to Norry Norris Fruit Bean, he was still feeling bad about sneaking the muffins out of the house.

Charlie Blue Berry Fipple Berry knew that he would have to tell his mother when he got home about where all the muffins disappeared to, and Charlie Blue Berry Fipple Berry was not going lie to his mother. Charlie Blue berry Fipple Berry's Mother and Father taught him never to lie, but always speak the truth.

Charlie Blue Berry Fipple Berry was feeling so bad about sneaking those extra muffins into his pocket that he wished he could run home to tell his Mother but he would be so late for school, so he would have to wait until he got home.

All morning at school, Charlie Blue Berry Fipple Berry sat by the window with such a sad face. The other kids played, and laughed and had fun on their last day of school, but not Charlie Blue berry Fipple Berry.

Then the sound that the kids had been waiting on all day was sounding.

CLANG . . . . CLANG . . . CLANG

The school bell rang!!!

Mr. Too Sweet Wise . . . The Lemon Berry Elementary School teacher said . . . . this is the last day of school kids!!!!

Remember to have fun be safe and grow up proud!!!

See to it to teach other people what you have learned all year and always tell the truth and do the right thing, that will make me so proud.

All the way home Norry Norris Fruit Bean skipped and wobbled, and belched and skipped and wobbled . . . .

Charlie Blue Berry Fipple Berry walked home with his hands in his pockets, still feeling the crumbs from the Blue Berry muffins in his pockets as he grabbed onto Norry Norris Fruit Bean's tail to keep up.

Charlie Blue Berry Fipple Berry, tried turning his pockets inside out so that the crumbs from the Blue Berry muffins would fall out, but nothing would take away the fresh, sweet smell of Blue Berry muffins, or what Charlie Blue Berry Fipple Berry was feeling.

Charlie Blue Berry Fipple Berry was still not happy; all the way home all he thought about was what his mother was going to say to him for sneaking all those Blueberry muffins this morning.

Norry Norris Fruit Bean said . . . . "Cheer up buddy, once you get home, take a nap, get up eat supper and you will be feeling super. Norry Norris Fruit Bean looked over to Charlie Blue Berry Fipple Berry and asked him . . . ." can I please borrow one of your fishing poles?

Charlie Blue Berry Fipple Berry are we still going fishing in the morning, in the morning, fishing??

Charlie Blue Berry Fipple Berry, shook his head yeah . . . I guess so Norry Norry.

The closer to Muffinville they grew, the more Norry Norris Fruit Bean started to run because he knew that his Mother would be making a supper soon, and boy was Norry Norris Fruit Bean hungry. Charlie Blue Berry Fipple Berry walked slower and slower worrying about what his Mother was going to say to him.

Charlie Blue Berry Fipple Berry thought about walking around to the back of his house to see if he could peek in the window, and see if his mother was cooking or doing something in the kitchen . . . maybe she was taking a nap and he could sneak in and run up to his room without his Mother seeing him.

Just then . . . . Charlie Blue Berry Fipple Berry saw his mother open the door and walking towards him.

Charlie Blue Berry Fipple Berry just hung his head down low, he knew he had to tell his Mother, he did not know when would be the right time to tell her, or if she would be upset with him. All Charlie Blue Berry Fipple Berry could think about was what kind of look would be on her face!

Charlie Blue Berry Fipple Berry was so scared, the only time he was this scared was when he wiped Blue Berry Stains on his Mother's new White Easter dress that she was wearing to the annual Easter Pageant show. That day his Mother was upset with Charlie Blue Berry Fipple Berry. His Mother had asked Charlie Blue Berry Fipple Berry to bring her dress down to the town hall so that she could change into it, and Charlie had Blue Berry stains all over the back of the dress and his mother did not know about the stains until she was walking on stage and people were laughing about it.

Charlie Blue Berry Fipple Berry looked up and his mother was standing in front of him . . . .

Charlie's Mother said . . . "how was the last day of school Charlie"?

Before Charlie Blue Berry Fipple Berry could answer her question . . . . his Mother reached down, picked up Charlie Blue Berry Fipple Berry, and gave him a big hug and a kiss.

"Oh Charlie, I am so proud of you . . . . finishing "little one's school son, you have made me so proud". Charlie Blue Berry Fipple Berry looked at his Mother and said . . . . Momma, I have to tell you something, this morning when you were going upstairs, I took more muffins from the pan when you told me not to.

His Mother looked at Charlie Blue Berry Fipple Berry and a big smile came over her face, she said' Charlie, thanks for telling me.

I'm not upset with you Charlie, but I told you those Blue Berry Muffins were for Mrs. Fruit Jelly Goose, and I had to make a new pan full, because you did what I asked you not to.

I am happy that you told the truth Charlie, but you are going to have to learn to do the right thing. When I tell you something, I expect for you to listen and obey. Charlie's Mother was not as upset as Charlie Blue Berry Fipple Berry thought. Charlie's Mother said, "As punishment for what you did this morning, I baked a Double Blue Berry pie and you will not be getting any for desert.

Charlie Blue Berry Fipple Berry, looked up at his
Mother and said . . . .
"I understand Momma, and I'm sorry".

Charlie's Mother took hold of Charlie's hand as they
walked home and said . . .
"how was your last day at school Charlie?

Charlie Blue Berry Fipple Berry . . . said, just fine
Momma, It was fine Momma.

Charlie Blue Berry Fipple Berry's Mother said, after we eat a real special supper your father and I have a special surprise for you. Now I want you to go in and wash your hands and change out of your school clothes, supper will be ready soon.

After a supper of Blueberry muffins, and Blueberry pie and Blueberries on the side, Charlie Blue Berry Fipple Berry and his Mother and Father sat Charlie Blue Berry Fipple Berry down to tell him about his surprise.

Charlie Blue Berry Fipple Berry's Mother and Father began to tell Charlie Blue Berry Fipple Berry, how he has always wanted someone to play with and that tomorrow, when the moon has a blue ring around it that Charlie Blue Berry Fipple Berry would have a new baby brother.

Charlie Blue Berry Fipple Berry was real sad, and began to cry . . . . his mother asked Charlie what was wrong, and Charlie Blue Berry Fipple Berry said "I don't want you and Daddy to put me back in the Blue Berry patch, I like it here, and I will promise to be really good from now on, I promise."

His Mother and Father told Charlie Blue Berry Fipple Berry not to worry, he is and will always be their son, and that they love him with all the love in their hearts.

Charlie Blue berry Fipple Berry asked his Mother and Father, why are they going to go to the Blue Berry Patch and get another son if they love him so much?

His Mother and Father sat Charlie down and told him in Sweet Smellums when two people are husband and wife and when they love one another, to show the world their love they must leave a part of themselves behind, and the more they leave the more they loved one another.

Charlie Blue Berry Fipple Berry kissed and hugged his Mother and Father good night, and started his walk upstairs to his bedroom . . . .

As the night went on, Charlie Blue Berry Fipple Berry sat in his room looking at his bed, his dresser, his tooth brush, his clothes, and his toys . . . he started saying to himself . . . . This is my room, and my things and if another little one comes, there will not be enough things to share, and enough space to share, so I bet that Momma and Daddy are going to have to put me back in the Blue berry Patch.

Charlie Blue Berry Fipple Berry was feeling so bad, that he fell asleep and began dreaming . . . .

Charlie Blue Berry Fipple Berry began dreaming that his Mother and Father had found a new son, one that wouldn't make mistakes and they sent Charlie Blue Berry Fipple Berry back to the Blueberry patch.

When Charlie Blue Berry Fipple Berry woke up, he was thinking about the dream he had became afraid that his dream would come true. Charlie Blue Berry Fipple Berry put on his Blue Jacket, Red Scarf and left the house.

Before the Sea Grass Swallows began to whistle, Norry Norris Fruit Bean was walking to Charlie Blue Berry Fipple Berry's to pick him up so they could go fishing, but Charlie Blue Berry Fipple Berry was already gone.

Norry Norris Fruit Bean went down to Red Cider Apple Bush hill, their favorite fishing spot, Blue Berry Slush pond looking for Charlie Blue Berry Fipple Berry.

Norry Norris looked but did not see Charlie Blue Berry Fipple Berry!

Norry Norris Fruit Bean looked at Ousey Bousey Mousey's barn, but Charlie Blue Berry Fipple Berry was not there!

Norry Norris Fruit Bean looked in the Strawberry Baseball Fields, but Charlie Blue Berry Fipple Berry was not there!

Norry Norris Fruit Bean looked on the Peach Berry Football field, but Charlie Blue Berry Fipple Berry was not there!

Norry Norris Fruit Bean looked everywhere he could think of, he did not find Charlie Blue Berry Fipple Berry anywhere.

Norry Norris Fruit Bean thought he would go back to Charlie Blue Berry Fipple Berry's house, maybe Charlie Blue Berry Fipple Berry would be there.

As Norry Norris Fruit Bean got close to Charlie Blue Berry Fipple Berry's house he saw Charlie Blue Berry Fipple Berry's Father, coming towards him.

Any luck finding Charlie Blue Berry Fipple Berry, his dad cried?

No Mr. Grape Nuts Fipple Berry, I checked in our favorite hiding places, and Charlie Blue Berry Fipple Berry is nowhere to be found.

Mr. Grape Nuts Fipple Berry told Norry Norris Fruit
Bean he was getting worried about Charlie Blue Berry
Fipple Berry because the sky was starting to get dark
and a storm was coming.

I am so worried about my son, said Mr. Grape Nuts Fipple Berry. Charlie Blue Berry Fipple Berry left before any of us got out of bed, and he didn't have any breakfast.

Do not worry Mr. Grape Nuts Fipple Berry, we will find Charlie Blue Berry Fipple Berry soon; he could not have gone too far.

Norry Norris Fruit Bean went to the left towards Peachville, and Mr. Grape Nuts Fipple Berry went to search in Muffinville.

Sweet Smellums has four parts to it.

Cranberry Corner, Muffinville, Peachville, and Ginger Snap Hollow.

Everyone who lived in Sweet Smellums was told never to go beyond Ginger Snap Hollow, because that is where the Thickets are, and bad things are in the Thickets.

Norry Norris Fruit Bean was heading to Peachville; he knew not to go past Gingersnap Hollow. On the other side of Gingersnap Hollow are the beginnings of the Thickets. If you go past Gingersnap hollow you would never know you were in the Thickets until it was too late.

Norry Norris Fruit Bean was crying out for Charlie
Blue Berry Fipple Berry as loud as he could. The wind
was blowing really hard and soon the storm would
be here. When it rains, the rain water opens up the
ground and the Oogies come out, leaving really big
holes. When the Oogies leave the ground they leave big
holes and you could fall in and not be able to get out.

"CHARLIE . . . . BLUE BERRY FIPPLE BERRY!!! CHARLIE, CHARLIE"!!! Norry Norris cried and cried.

Norry Norris Fruit Bean was on the ridge in Gingersnap Hollow looking all around when he spotted something caught in the Thickets.

Norry Norris Fruit Bean ran down the ridge, being careful where his paws were because he did not want to cross over into the Thickets.

Norry Norris Fruit Bean came to the beginning of the Thickets and saw something caught in it!

It was a bright red scarf; "it's Charlie . . . Charlie's scarf . . . . thought Norry Norris Fruit Bean."

Norry Norris Fruit Bean knew the scarf belonged to Charlie Blue Berry Fipple Berry. Norry Norris Fruit Bean gave Charlie Blue Berry Fipple Berry that scarf as a friendship present.

Norry Norris Fruit Bean was worried about Charlie Blue Berry Fipple Berry because nobody from Sweet Smellums had gone into the Thickets before and Charlie Blue Berry Fipple Berry was so little.

Norry Norris Fruit Bean knew he would have to go in the Thickets to get his best friend, and he knew he had to have help. So he ran as fast as he could to Peachville.

Norry Norris Fruit Bean stopped at Pumpkin Flats Lane to Mrs. Sweet Nectar's house. Norry Norris Fruit Bean began knocking on the door . . . "help me, help me"!

The door opened up and there in the doorway stood
Mrs. Sweet Nectar. Can I help you Norry Norris Fruit
Bean said Mrs. Sweet Nectar?

Yes you may Mrs. Sweet Nectar, Charlie Blue Berry
Fipple Berry is in the Thickets and I'm going in there
after him, please get this message to his Father please?

Mrs. Sweet Nectar grabbed her hat and umbrella and headed out to Muffinville to find Charlie's Father!.

Norry Norris Fruit Bean was running as fast as he could back to the Thickets. Norry Norris Fruit Bean was afraid of going in the Thickets, but he had to help his friend.

Norry Norris Fruit Bean grabbed Charlie Blue Berry
Fipple Berry's bright red scarf and tied it around
his neck. Norry Norris Fruit Bean started into the
Thickets and had to bend down low.

The Thickets are thick woods with sticky thorns
everywhere you walked. A person would get caught in
the Thickets because the thorns stick everywhere and
you would not be able to get out!

Slowly Norry Norris Fruit Bean went inside, looking left, and then looking right. Norry Norris Fruit Bean looked behind to see how far into the thickets he had gone.

Smaller and smaller the opening of the thickets got, which meant Norry Norris Fruit Bean was deep inside the Thickets. The wind was blowing and it started raining hard. Norry Norris Fruit Bean kept his head down to see through the rain.

If it had not been raining so hard, Norry Norris Fruit Bean would have been able to see Charlie Blue Berry Fipple Berry's tracks. Norry Norris Fruit Fruit Bean looked and saw Muddy Sad Sage Creek at the bottom of the hill. Norry Norris Fruit Fruit Bean hoped that his best friend had not slipped and fell into the creek.

Norry Norris Fruit Fruit Bean looked really hard and saw some small foot tracks ahead. They were little Hedgehog prints. they were Charlie Blue Berry Fipple Berry's tracks.

Slowly Norry Norris Fruit Bean kept following the tracks until the tracks stopped at Sad Sage Creek. Norry Norris Fruit Bean knew that his friend slipped into the muddy creek.

Sad Sage Creek was a very deep muddy creek that flowed all the way to the other side of the world. It was called Sad Sage because the fish, and frogs, and things that live in water would not swim in muddy creek. The Elves said it stays muddy all the time, even when it's not raining; and nothing can breathe in it.

Norry Norris Fruit Bean stood up on the hill looking all around Sad Sage Creek trying to see if he could see his friend.

Norry Norris Fruit Bean saw a little Blue Jacket floating in the creek, by some bushes. Norry Norris Fruit Bean took one step, and then another, trying hard not to go too fast so he would not slip into the creek.

Norry Norris Fruit Bean was a good swimmer, everyone knows the Polar Bears are very good swimmers. Norry Norris Fruit Bean got to the edge of the creek; he took Charlie Blue Berry Fipple Berry's Red scarf and tied it to a limb before he slid into Sad Sage Muddy Creek.

Norry Norris Fruit bean could not see in this muddy water, but his eyesight under water was better than the average Sweet Smellums eyesight on dry land. Norry Norris Fruit bean came up out of the water wiping his eyes and taking another deep breath before he went back down in the muddy water. Just when Norry Norris Fruit bean thought he'd never see his friend again, he saw Charlie Blue Berry Fipple Berry, caught in weeds and going down stream.

Norry Norris Fruit bean knew that the only way to save Charlie Blue Berry Fipple Berry was to swim over to him, but Norry Norris needed to get a really big deep breath first.

When Norry Norris Fruit bean came to the top of Sad Sage creek to get a breath, he saw Charlie Blue Berry Fipple Berry's father on the bank of the creek. Mr. Grape Nuts Fipple Berry cried out . . . "have you found Charlie Blue Berry Fipple Berry . . . . have you found him Norry Norris Fruit Bean ?"

Norry Norris Fruit bean yelled back, I see him, but I'll need your help . . . . The storm and the muddy waters are making it hard to see, and if I grab Charlie Blue Berry Fipple Berry, I won't know which way the bank and start is heading down into the water.

Okay cried Mr. Fipple Berry, what if I tie Charlie Blue Berry Fipple Berry's scarf around your tail, and I grab hold to this tree? Norry Norris Fruit bean Nodded and swam over to Charlie Blue Berry Fipple Berry's father. He tied Charlie Blue Berry Fipple Berry's scarf around Norry Norris Fruit bean tail and back into the water Norry Norris Fruit bean went.

After two or three minutes Norry Norris Fruit bean came up out of the water with Charlie Blue Berry Fipple Berry in his mouth.

Charlie Blue Berry Fipple Berry's father began pulling onto Charlie Fipple Berry's scarf which was tied around Norry Norris Fruit bean tail. Mr. Grape Nuts Fipple Berry crawled back up the muddy hill, slipping and sliding down again and again. Finally Mr. Grape Nuts Fipple Berry made it to the top and tied Charlie Blue Berry Fipple Berry's scarf around a tree.

Norry Norris Fruit Bean stretched out his huge claws and dug deep into the mud to make it up the hill, but the storm was very bad and even Norry Norris Fruit bean big claws were no match for the muddy hill.

Mr. Fipple Berry called out to Norry Norris Fruit bean . . . . "Norry Norris Fruit Bean, can you make it? But Norry Norris Fruit bean knew that if he did not have Charlie Blue Berry Fipple Berry by his suspenders in his mouth he could make it by grabbing onto branches and limbs with his large teeth to help pull him up.

Norry Norris Fruit Bean slid backwards once, then again, then again.

Norry Norris Fruit Bean knew the only way to save his friend and to make it back up the hill was to use all his strength and throw Charlie Blue Berry Fipple Berry Fipple Berry up on the top of the hill.

Charlie's father saw Norry Norris Fruit Bean putting his head down and swinging back and forth, back and forth and knew Norry Norris Fruit Bean was going to try to throw Charlie Blue Berry Fipple Berry Fipple Berry on on top of the hill, so he climbed up to wait on Norry Norris Fruit Bean.

Then with all the strength that Norry Norris Fruit Bean had, He threw Charlie Blue Berry Fipple Berry as hard as he could. Charlie Blue Berry Fipple Berry flew in the air up the hill and landed in his father's arms.

Charlie's Father was hugging and kissing Charlie Blue Berry Fipple Berry, and then looked back at Norry Norris Fruit Bean who was slowly climbing the up hill. "Do you need any help Norris" . . . shouted Charlie's Father?

No I am alright Norry Norris Fruit Bean said, just get Charlie Blue Berry Fipple Berry home, it's starting to get really dark, and the Oogies will be coming out soon.

Alright cried Charlie's Father, he tucked Charlie Blue Berry Fipple Berry in his arms and began making his way through the Thickets.

Charlie's Father was so happy to have Charlie Blue Berry Fipple Berry safe, that he forgot Norry Norris Fruit Bean was still climbing up the hill from Sad Sage Creek.

Norry Norris Fruit Bean was 400 pounds, and that made it hard trying to climb up a muddy hill.

The hill was really slippery, every time Norry Norris Fruit Bean took one step up the hill he would slide down again. Norry Norris Fruit Bean put his sharp claws into the mud and began climbing the hill.

All Norry Norris Fruit Bean had to do was reach out with his teeth to grab onto this branch, and pull himself up on top of the hill.

Norry Norris Fruit Bean could see Charlie's Father carrying Charlie Blue Berry Fipple Berry out of the Thickets. Norry Norris Fruit Bean thought to himself . . . . "when I get out of this Creek I will run fast and catch up with them in no time",

Norry Norris Fruit Bean was tired from all the swimming and Climbing, that when he reached out to grab the last branch and pull and dig his claws in the muddy hill, that lightening struck the tree and the branch broke off from the tree and Norry Norris Fruit Bean slid back down into the muddy water, under the water Norry Norris went.

The big tree came out of the ground and was sliding down into the creek behind Norry Norris Fruit Bean. All of a sudden two big muddy paws came out of the water and tried to get on shore, but the big Oak tree came down on top of Norry Norris Fruit Bean, knocking him back into the water.

Charlie's Father made it all the way back through Peachville to Muffinville without seeing any Oogies. Charlie Blue Berry Fipple Berry was safe.

Charlie's Mother, was standing in the door waiting when they arrived. She cried for all of Muffinville to come and help them celebrate that Charlie Blue Berry Fipple Berry was safe.

All the people who lived in Sweet Smellums came over to Charlie Blue Berry Fipple Berry's house and bought all kinds of food, and music and games to have a party for Charlie Blue Berry Fipple Berry.

Charlie Blue Berry Fipple Berry was so happy, that all the people came to wish him well. The person Charlie Blue Berry Fipple Berry wanted to see the most was Norry Norris Fruit Bean. Charlie's Father told him that it was Norry Norris Fruit Bean who went into the Thickets to save him.

Charlie Blue Berry Fipple Berry felt something cold and wet on his arm and turned around and it was Norry Norris Fruit Bean.

Norry Norris Fruit Bean told Charlie Blue Berry Fipple Berry . . . "you are my friend Charlie Blue Berry Fipple Berry. Norry Norris Fruit Bean told Charlie Blue Berry Fipple Berry, "after I helped your Father get you out of the water I slipped back down into the water and almost drowned.

It was the Elves Charlie Blue Berry Fipple Berry, the Elves. The Elves lifted me out of the water and carried me all the way to Muffinville. They told me, when you are doing the right thing and you get in trouble well, they will always be there to help us, and they will be watching to see the good that we do.

Charlie Blue Berry Fipple Berry said, "Norry, Norry, I am so glad to have you as my friend.

The end.